tiger flower

tiger flower

by *Robert Vavra*

paintings by Fleur Cowles

PREFACE BY YEHUDI MENUHIN

REYNAL & COMPANY
in association with
William Morrow & Company, Inc.
New York

Published in Great Britain in 1968.
Published in the United States in 1969.
Printed in the United States of America.

Library of Congress Catalog Card Number 69-20105

The child's world is a world of symbols, shapes and sizes until that dismal day when it is taught to put a label on each and every thing it has felt, touched and smelt, and forced to shrink it by a name.

The child's world is the poet's world where dimensions differ only according to feeling, not fact, that place of the fourth dimension that eludes all but painters, poets, lunatics and the players of musical instruments. And it even eludes those at times. That is why they remain children, eternally commited to chasing after it, clinging to the tatters of those clouds of glory with which we are all born and which only rationalisation can rip off.

Definitions are dull and delineations even duller. Blake's Tiger would never have burnt bright in the forests of an adult's night, but simply have gone out like a light while the adult died of fright.

But beautiful things are not fearful in the innocent world because there one has curiosity instead of terror and a suppleness of mind that adjusts itself to the wonder of the unexpected as easily as the pupil of the eye to the fluctuations of light and dark.

Here then is a little book that is the right way up. A glimpse of a world wherein there is so much time and limitless space that no one has to confine or categorise out of meanness of heart, for fear that there won't be enough beauty or enough truth to go around unless you frighten others away.

Yehudi Menuhin

One day a bird flew to the grass
where everything that should be small,
is big.
And everything that should be big,
is small.

The bird saw
a tiny tiger
in the grass

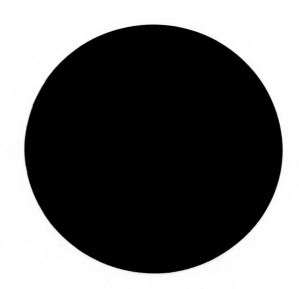

and twittered,

the jungle that lies
beyond the mountain,

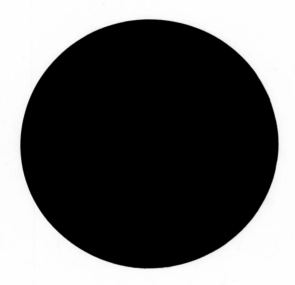

where everything is
the way it should be.

"SILENCE!!!"
growled the tiny tiger.
"The grass!
The grass !
The tall,
tall grass.
Tiger Flower,
King of the Grass,
that's me.

Once I was king of the scarey,
towering,
tangled
green jungle
where tigers are
big
and the way they should be.
I growled
and roared
and snarled
and ground my teeth
and frightened all the other animals
and outsmarted the hunters.
What work it was
being big
and mean
and crafty.
You're lucky I'm not there
or grrrrrrrrrrrrrrrrrrrrrrrrrrr,
I'd be hunting you
instead of flowers.

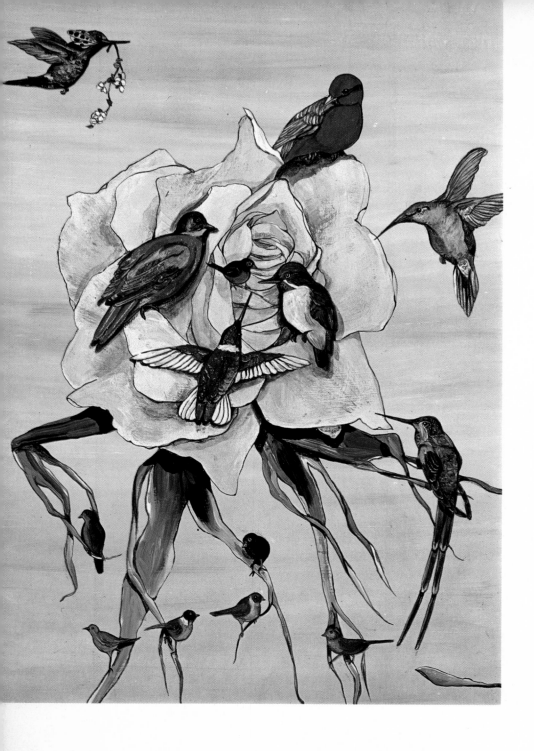

Until the wild wind came,
everything was the way
it should have been in the jungle.
The birds sat idly about,
twittering and tweeping
like you.

And the butterflies
did nothing but
pop,
split,
crackle out of their
chrysalises
and sit around
on the ground,
showing off their wings.

Then
zoooooom,
whhhisssssssh,
phffffffffffffffft
came the wind.
The jungle had never known
such a wild,
wild wind.
It swept away
leaves
and branches
and even nests.

It picked up
insects
and birds
and whole clods of earth.
And carried them off
fast
and high
and
far
away.

The butterflies
who always complained
about being so
small
and
soooooo delicate,
and who sat all day,
all night,
all afternoon,
showing off
in the jungle,
found themselves
trying to grab
onto branches
flung through
space.

Even the big animals and birds
could do nothing
but hang on
and look surprised.
Some stomped their
hoofs
and ground their
teeth
and bellowed
and roared.
But it did
no good.

Sailing,
sailing,
all of us
were sailing
until we
reached

the tall,
tall
grass
where everything that should be small,
is big,
and everything that should be big,
is small.

I lit
on a blade of grass.
A tiger
on a blade of grass!
Ho-ho,
har-har,
ha-ha.
And I've been here
happily ever since,
where mushrooms are bigger
than trees.
Where everything
is turned around.
Where nothing
is the way it should be
or
the way it once was.

Now,
the butterflies,
because they're
big,
sail boats
and use their wings
for more than show.

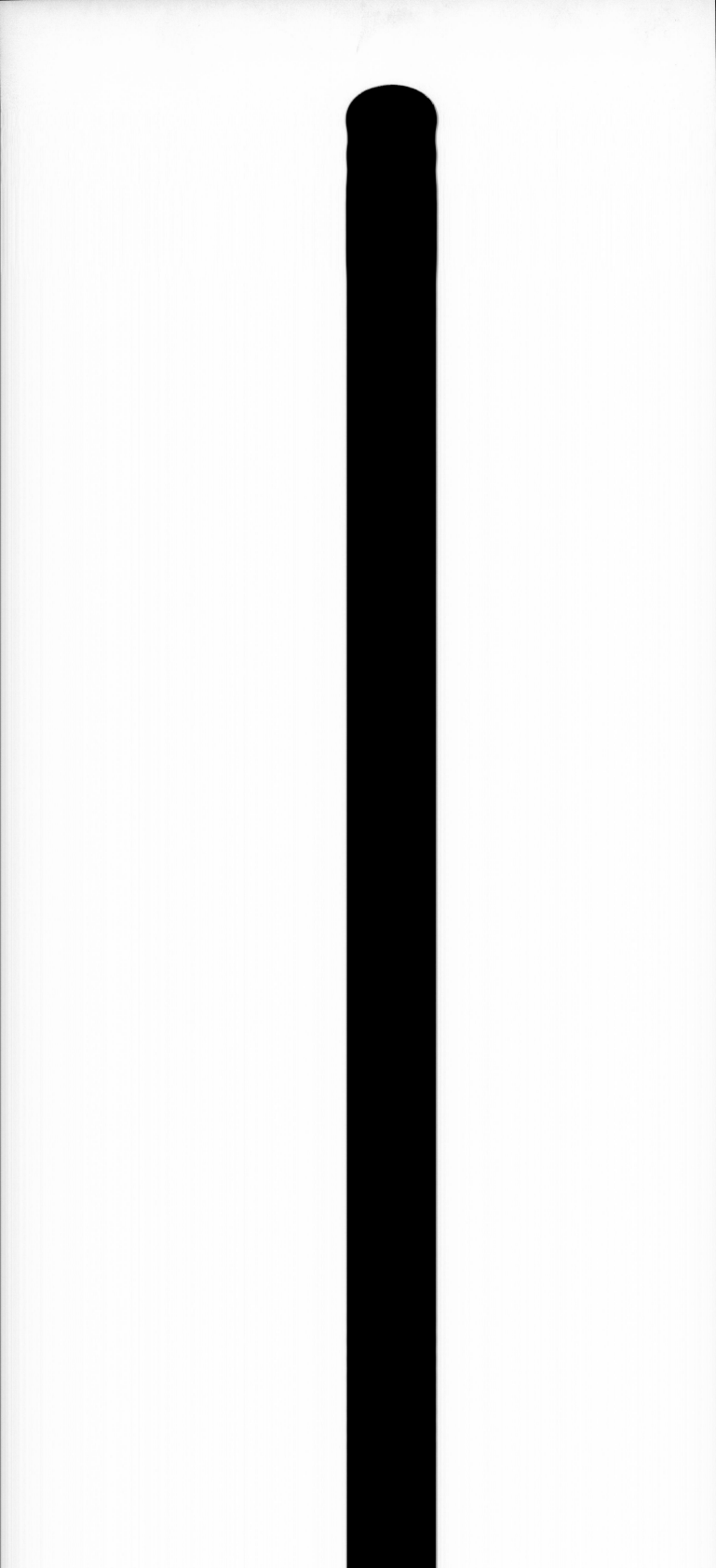

The birds are his
friends
and not his
dinner.
And instead of hunting
zebra,

he hunts
flowers.
How happy
he is.

Here,
cheetahs
chase
nothing
but shadows
on the beach.
And
elephants
uproot
flowers
only for
their crowns.

You see,
if you're born
a jungle beast
you have to be
big
and
fierce
the way jungle beasts
are supposed to be
or life becomes
unpleasant for you.
Here,
where nothing is
as it should
be,
no one has to be
anyway but
the way
he is.

Instead of seeking out
a den
of boulders,
the cheetah makes his cubs
a nest
of leaves.

And when my friends
and I
tire of gathering
flowers
we go for a ride
across a lake
that is always
smooth.

*And I never have to worry
about guns.*

Only
flower
hunters
who sometimes carry me off
in their
bouquets.
But I always find
my way home.

So,
grrrrrrrrrrrrrrrrrrrr,
big bird,
silly bird,
bird like every other
bird,
now if you wish,
fly back beyond the mountain
where things are the way
they are supposed to be.
Where tigers snarl
and lions roar
and cheetahs growl
and elephants trumpet
and butterflies and birds
do
nothing at all.

And sing
to the towering,
tangled
green jungle
that you've been here
where everyone is just
himself,
even me,
a silly,
tiny
tiger
with a flower
between my teeth —
in the grass!

The grass!
The grass!
The tall,
tall grass!
Tiger Flower,
King of the Grass.
That's me!"

OWNERSHIP OF PAINTINGS

PAINTINGS		FROM THE COLLECTION OF
Cover		*H.E. Ambassador and Mrs Angier Biddle Duke*
African Sunset	*page 8*	*Mr and Mrs Ronald Grierson, London*
Tall Grass	*page 11*	*Mr & Mrs John Alex McCone, California*
Silver Birch	*pp 12–13*	*Miss Helen Lee, New York*
Rose Sanctuary	*page 14*	*Mr John Sossidi, Athens*
Flower in Flight	*page 15*	*Mr & Mrs Stanley Arnold, New York*
Floating Log	*page 16*	*Mr Edwin Daniels, London*
Afloat	*page 17*	*Mr & Mrs Justin Dart, Beverly Hills*
Autumn Flight	*page 19*	*Mr & Mrs Townsend B. Martin, New York*
Day Flight	*page 21*	*Mrs Lillian Steele, New York*
Tree Irises	*pp 22–23*	*Mr & Mrs William Goetze, San Francisco*
Magic Mushrooms	*page 24*	*Col James A. Carreras M.B.E. & Mrs Carreras, London*
Tiger in the Grass	*page 25*	*Mr & Mrs Tom Montague Meyer, London*
Flower Sail	*page 26*	*Princess Marina Orloff, New York*
Lion among the Birds	*page 29*	*Mrs Robert M. Blake, Connecticut*
Zebra Crossing	*pp 30-31*	*Mme Hélène Vlakou, Athens*
Waiting	*page 33*	*T.M. King Constantine & Queen Anne-Marie of Greece*
Day by the Sea	*page 34*	*Mr & Mrs Enrico Donati, New York*
Loving Couple	*page 35*	*Mr A. Rother, Montreal*
Family Portrait	*pp 36–37*	*Mr Ely R. Callaway Jr, Connecticut*
Romantic Interlude	*page 39*	*Mrs Jay Holmes, Beverly Hills*
Resting Place	*page 40*	*Prof. Stratis Andreadis, Athens*
Tiger on a Blade	*page 42*	*Dr Walter Willard Boyd, Washington, D. C.*
Crowned Tiger	*page 44*	*H.E. Ambassador and Mrs Angier Biddle Duke*

AUTHOR'S NOTE

When I first saw Fleur Cowles's paintings in London, I was convinced they would make wonderful illustrations for a book. They had a rare imaginative quality about them that filled me with instant enthusiasm for such a project. But Fleur is an internationally known painter, not an illustrator, and I knew that she, like many painters, might not consent to illustrating someone else's ideas. So that same evening, not wanting to leave her creatures behind me for ever, I proposed that she send me about eighty photographs of paintings she had done. And because she has an adventurous artistic spirit, one that knows few boundaries, she agreed.

In the months that followed, small packages of photographs of these paintings reached me in Spain. They came from collections in Greece and France and South America and Italy and the United States and Australia and many other places. Fleur did not have an easy job tracking them down. But she did it. Then, all laid out on my work table, those that appear in this book rapidly fell into order. It was not the ordinary way of making such a book—illustrations before text. But then, Fleur's tiger was not a very ordinary cat.

Robert Vavra